The Pug who wanted to be a Bumblebee

Text by Anne Marie Ryan.

Illustrations by Nina Jones and Artful Doodlers.

ORCHARD BOOKS

First published in Great Britain in 2023 by Hodder & Stoughton

1 3 5 7 9 10 8 6 4 2

A CIP catalogue record for this book
is available from the British Library.

ISBN 978 1 40837 130 5

Printed and bound in Great Britain by Clays Ltd, Elcograf S.p.A.
The paper and board used in this book are made from wood from responsible sources.

Orchard Books
An imprint of
Hachette Children's Group
Part of Hodder & Stoughton
Carmelite House
50 Victoria Embankment
London EC4Y 0DZ

An Hachette UK Company
www.hachette.co.uk
www.hachettechildrens.co.uk

The Pug who wanted to be a Bumblebee

Bella Swift

Contents

Chapter One

"Let's play!" Peggy barked, dropping a tennis ball by Dad's feet in the garden. To him, it just sounded like "woof", but Peggy hoped that if she wagged her curly little tail hard enough he'd understand.

"Sorry, Pegs," said Dad, scratching

the pug behind her floppy ears. "I've got strawberries to pick." He twisted a plump red berry off the vine and added it to his bowl.

Dad took great pride in his garden. On sunny days, he was often out there weeding, mowing the lawn and watering his fruit and vegetables. Peggy was strictly forbidden from digging holes among the neat rows of plants, even though the soil was the perfect place to bury a bone. You never knew when you'd feel a bit peckish, after all . . .

As she trotted away with her ball

Peggy saw Tiger, the stripy ginger cat who lived next door, sunbathing on the roof of the garden shed.

"Hey, Tiger," she called up to him hopefully. "Want to—"

"No, I do not want to play with you, Pig Tail,"  he interrupted, his green eyes opening to glare at her. "I am taking a nap. Or at least TRYING to take a nap." Tiger stretched his furry ginger body, rolled over and went back to sleep.

Peggy sighed. Tiger was such a grump.

"I'll play with you, Peggy," called a soft voice from across the garden.

Peggy bounded over the grass, past flower beds blooming with lavender, hollyhocks and snapdragons, and over to a wooden rabbit hutch.

"Hi, Coco," she said, pressing her flat black nose against the wire screen to greet the black and white rabbit inside the hutch.

"Let's play I Spy," suggested Coco.

"Sure," said Peggy. Coco always

wanted to play I Spy. "You can go first."

The bunny twitched her nose. "I spy with my little eye something beginning with 'C' . . ."

"Is it a carrot?" guessed Peggy.

"Yes!" said Coco, sounding amazed. "How did you know?"

"Lucky guess," said Peggy. It was usually a carrot. Or a radish. Or some hay. It wasn't Coco's fault – there wasn't much to see inside her hutch.

"I've got another one," said Coco, her fluffy tail twitching. "I spy something else beginning with 'C' . . ."

"Cabbage," guessed Peggy.

"No," said the bunny. "It's Chloe!"

Spinning around, Peggy saw Chloe, Ruby and Finn step through the patio doors into the garden. The children were home from school! With an excited bark, Peggy ran straight to Chloe and jumped into her best friend's outstretched arms.

Peggy loved all three children in her family, but she'd had a special bond with Chloe ever since they first met.

"I missed you when I was at school, Peggy," Chloe said, stroking Peggy's soft tan-coloured fur.

"I missed you too," said Peggy, licking

her friend's cheek.

"I missed you too," said Peggy. But to Chloe it just sounded like barking.

"Is there anything to eat, Dad?" asked Finn, Chloe's older brother. Like Peggy, he was ALWAYS hungry.

"Freshly picked strawberries," said Dad, standing up and brushing dirt off his knees. He came over to the patio and offered the children the bowl of fruit. "How was school?"

"We're having a science fair at the end of term," said Chloe, reaching for a berry. "I'm doing a project with Ellie and Hannah."

Peggy knew those were Chloe's human best friends.

"What's your project going to be on?" asked Ruby, Chloe's little sister. Her lips were stained red with strawberry juice.

"We haven't decided yet," said Chloe.

"They're coming over next weekend so we can plan it."

"I built that for my science fair project," said Finn, pointing to a robot in the garden. "I got an A plus."

Peggy eyed the robot suspiciously. Its solar-powered arms moved to frighten a bird away like a scarecrow. But it was also good at scaring dogs away.

"I really want to get a good grade too," said Chloe. She put her hands over Peggy's ears and lowered her voice to a whisper. "I want to be a vet when I grow up. You need to be good at science to do that."

I heard that, thought Peggy, even though Chloe had covered her ears. Peggy hated going to the vet. It usually meant getting jabbed with a needle. As much as she loved Chloe, she couldn't understand why her friend wanted to do such a horrible job. Chloe was much too nice to be a vet!

As Dad and the children ate the strawberries, they brainstormed ideas for Chloe's science fair project.

"You could build a robot like I did," said Finn.

No! thought Peggy. One scary robot was enough.

"Yeah!" said Ruby. "Make a robot that can do homework." She bit into a big strawberry and juice dribbled down her chin.

Peggy's mouth watered as she watched the children eat. She whined, hoping for a snack.

"Do you want one too, Peggy?" Chloe asked, giving her a strawberry.

Yum! thought Peggy, wolfing it down.

"There was a Russian scientist named Pavlov who did a very famous experiment a long time ago," said Dad. "He rang a bell before feeding his dogs and noticed that they started drooling as soon as they heard the bell."

"You could recreate that experiment," said Finn. "I'm sure Peggy would help."

"Yes!" barked Peggy. She liked the

sound of extra treats, especially if it meant helping Chloe.

"Aaaaarggghhh!" shrieked Ruby, jumping up and hiding behind Dad.

"What's wrong?" Dad asked.

BZZZZZZ . . . BZZZZZZ. . . BZZZZZZ. A fluffy black and yellow bee buzzed around the bowl of strawberries.

"Bee!" Ruby squealed. "It's going to sting me!"

"Hold still and stop shouting, and it'll go away," said Dad.

The buzzing bee flew away and landed on a daisy.

"You shouldn't be scared of bees," Finn told his sister. "Bees are amazing. I've been learning all about them in biology. They are some of the most important creatures in the whole world."

"Why?" asked Chloe.

"Because if it wasn't for them, we wouldn't have food crops to eat," said Finn.

Wow, thought Peggy, watching the bee buzz from flower to flower. She'd had no idea these tiny creatures were so impressive.

"Unfortunately, bees are endangered," said Finn. "They like to live in wildflower meadows – but there aren't so many of those any more."

"Poor bees," said Ruby sadly.

Peggy felt sorry for the bees too. She remembered what it was like not to have a home, before Chloe's family adopted her from the dog shelter.

"We should get a beehive," said Chloe. "There are plenty of flowers for them in our garden."

"Hmm . . ." said Dad thoughtfully. "That's an interesting idea . . ."

"I could build a hive," volunteered Finn.

Just then, Mum came home.

"Guess what?" said Chloe as Mum joined them on the patio. "We're going to get a beehive."

"To save the bees!" cried Ruby.

"Ooh!" said Mum excitedly. "I can

sell jars of honey in the café." Mum owned a dog-friendly café called Pups and Cups in the town centre. "And I know lots of recipes that have honey in the ingredients. Speaking of which, I brought some honey and spice cake back from the café. Does anyone want a piece?"

"Me!" said Finn.

"Me too!" said Chloe.

"And me!" said Ruby.

Mmm! thought Peggy. She watched the children hopefully as they helped themselves to cake.

"Here you go," said Chloe, breaking

off a bit of cake for Peggy, just as Peggy knew she would. Chloe *always* shared her treats with Peggy. And if getting bees meant getting more treats, Peggy couldn't wait for them to arrive!

Chapter Two

"Can't you come to the farm with us, Mummy?" asked Ruby.

"I wish I could," said Mum. "But I've got to go to the café. Saturday is our busiest day."

"We'll bring you home some honey," said Chloe, giving Mum a kiss goodbye.

"Can you get me some eggs from the farm shop as well?" said Mum. "I'll make mushroom omelettes for dinner."

Yum, thought Peggy.

"Hurry up, Finn," Dad called up the stairs. "We're leaving soon."

Finn came downstairs, his hair still tousled from bed. Then Dad, the kids and Peggy got in the car and set off. As they drove out of town, soon the streets of houses were replaced by green fields and hedgerows full of chirping birds. Peggy stuck her head out of the window, her ears flapping in the breeze as she breathed in the fresh country air.

"Pee-yew!" moaned Chloe, holding her nose. "It stinks."

Peggy thought it smelled nice.

"That's the manure farmers spread on the soil to make their plants grow," explained Dad.

"Manure means POO!" Finn told Ruby.

"Ewww!" Ruby wrinkled her nose and pulled a disgusted face.

Dad turned down a long gravel drive with a farmhouse and several barns at the end. "Here we are."

"Welcome to Honey Valley Farm," said a man wearing a big white suit, gloves and a hat with a mesh veil. "I'm Mr Apis."

"Why are you dressed like an astronaut?" asked Ruby.

Mr Apis chuckled. "This is my beekeeping suit," he said.

"I'll need to get one of those," said Dad.

"Let me show you around," said Mr Apis.

They walked down a dirt path. On one side there were fields filled with animals grazing, and on the other side there were vegetable crops – rows of leafy lettuces, peas and carrots.

Coco would love it here, thought Peggy.

"This is an organic farm," explained Mr Apis. "I don't use any pesticides on my plants, because chemicals hurt bees and other insects."

"We need to save the bees!" said Ruby.

"That's right," said Mr Apis, patting her on the head.

Peggy heard the steady hum of the beehives before she saw them. There were six wooden boxes in a row at the edge of the field. Bees flew back and forth between the hives and the fields.

"Each hive holds several thousand bees," said Mr Apis.

Peggy's ears pricked up with excitement. Soon there would be lots more animals for her to play with at home!

"What are the bees doing?" asked Chloe.

"They're sucking up nectar from flowers and bringing it back to the hive," explained Mr Apis.

Mr Apis opened the hive and pulled out a wooden frame covered in bees. He brushed the bees off with his gloved hand. Underneath there was a layer of honeycomb, made from wax.

"Over time, the warm breeze made by the bees' wings beating inside the hive turns the nectar into honey," said Mr Apis. "The bees cover the honey with wax to store it."

Wow, thought Peggy. Making honey sounded like a lot of work. No wonder the bees looked so busy! She decided not to disturb them.

While Mr Apis answered everyone's questions about beekeeping, Peggy headed over to the pasture, hoping to make some new friends.

"Hi," she called to a speckled hen

pecking in the
soil. "What
are you
doing?"

"I'm
looking for
a hiding
place for my
eggs," said the
chicken.

"Ooh!" said Peggy. "That sounds fun.
Can I play too?" Hide and seek was
one of her favourite games!

"Fun?" clucked the chicken
indignantly, peering at Peggy with a

black, beady eye. "This is not a game. Laying eggs is a very important job." The hen waddled off, tutting.

"Sorry!" Peggy called after her. She hadn't meant to offend the chicken.

In the next field along, some cows were munching clover. Peggy stared at the one closest to the fence. She had kind, long-lashed eyes, but Peggy kept her distance. She'd never met such a big creature before and she didn't want to get trampled!

"MOOOOO!" said the cow. "How do you dooooo?"

"I'm Peggy. Do you want to play?"

Peggy wagged her tail eagerly.

"No can doooooo, I'm afraid," said the cow. "It's milking time. I've got to get back to the barn."

The next pasture along was filled with sheep. The grown-ups were grazing, but the frisky little lambs were having lots of fun, leaping and frolicking across the meadow. Peggy wriggled under the fence to join them. "Can I play too?" she asked.

"Sure!" called a fluffy white lamb.

"You're it!" shouted a lamb with black spots on his fleece, butting Peggy with his head.

Yapping happily, Peggy chased after the lambs as they dodged and dived across the pasture. "Gotcha!" she said, tagging the spotty lamb with her paw.

Peggy and her new friends flopped on the grass for a rest. Peggy panted until she'd got her breath back.

"Thanks for letting me play. Everyone else was too busy," said Peggy. "The bees are busy making honey, the chickens are busy making eggs, the cows are busy making milk. I'm glad you lot are like me – we don't make anything."

"Baa haa haa!" laughed the lambs.

"What's so funny?" asked Peggy.

"Oh yes we do make something!" explained the white lamb. "Our fleece is very soft and warm. Humans use our wool to make clothes."

"Oh . . ." said Peggy, feeling embarrassed.

"PEGGY!" called Chloe.

"Gotta go!" barked Peggy with relief, racing across the field to join her family.

They followed Mr Apis to the farm shop, which was in an old barn made of stone. Inside, the shop sold products made on the farm. There were crates of vegetables, boxes of eggs, bottles of creamy milk, candles made of beeswax and of course jars of golden honey. Mr Apis took off his hat and introduced Peggy's family to his wife, who ran the shop.

"Would you like to try some of our honey?" Mrs Apis asked. She gave each of the children a lollipop made with honey.

"Yum!" said Ruby, taking a lick. "It

tastes really sweet."

"Honey has lots of other uses too," said Mrs Apis. "You can put it in tea or spread it on wounds to help them heal."

Dad arranged with Mr Apis to have some bees delivered the following week. Then he bought a jar of honey to take home.

"Right," he said to the kids. "We should be on our way or Ruby will be late for her ballet class."

We need to get eggs, thought Peggy, remembering what Mum had said earlier about making omelettes.

Trying to be helpful, she ran over to

the table displaying boxes of eggs.

"Come on, Pegs," called Dad, patting his thighs.

"Don't forget the eggs!" she barked. She tugged at the red and white checked tablecloth, trying to give Dad a clue.

A box of eggs slid off the table and fell on the floor.

CRACK!

Broken

eggshells and runny yellow yolks spilled everywhere.

Oh dear, thought Peggy.

"I'm so sorry," said Dad, hurrying over. "I don't know what's got into Peggy. Too much excitement, I guess."

I was just trying to be helpful, like all the other animals, thought Peggy.

"No worries," said Mrs Apis cheerfully, mopping up the mess. "Accidents happen."

"But that reminds me . . . my wife wanted me to buy some eggs," said Dad. He bought two boxes. "Now we really will be on our way."

"Bees are so cool!" said Chloe, licking her lollipop as they walked back to the car.

"Mmm," agreed Finn.

"This was fun," said Ruby, skipping along as she held Dad's hand.

Peggy's family was happy, but Peggy felt worried. All the animals she'd met today could make something – even the little lambs. But the only thing she was good at making was a mess!

Chapter Three

The sound of sawing and hammering
was coming from the garage, where
Finn was building a beehive. He'd been
working on it all week after school.
Going into the garage with Chloe
and Ruby, Peggy sniffed, inhaling the
deliciously woody smell of sawdust.

"How's it going?" asked Chloe.

"Nearly done," said Finn, twisting a screw into place with a screwdriver.

Chloe held out the bag of cheese puffs she was carrying. "Mum said you might need a snack."

"Thanks," said Finn. He dipped his hand in the bag and took out some cheese puffs, then passed the bag to his sisters.

Chloe helped herself to some cheese puffs, then touched a hole in the wood. "Is this the door?" she asked. Orange powder from her fingers rubbed off on the wood.

"Yes," said Finn. "But don't touch — you're getting orange stuff everywhere."

"That's how pollination works," said Chloe. "I've been reading all about it. When bees gather nectar, pollen from the flowers sticks to their legs, like the cheesy powder sticks to our fingers. Then, when they fly to the next flower, the pollen brushes off on it."

She offered her cheesy fingers to Peggy, who gladly licked the tasty powder off them.

"There isn't going to be anywhere for them to live if I don't get this hive finished," said Finn.

The girls left Finn to his work and went inside. Peggy heard Chloe's friends coming up the path before they even rang the doorbell.

"They're here!" she barked, announcing the visitors. When Chloe opened the door, Peggy was delighted to see that Hannah had brought along her terrier, Princess.

"Hi, Peggy!" yipped Princess, running inside to give her friend a sniff.

Wagging her tail excitedly, Peggy nuzzled Princess's nose. Princess loved to play as much as Peggy did!

"Aww!" said Ruby, crouching down

to pat Princess. "I love her outfit. She's a ballerina like me."

Princess was wearing a pink tutu and a matching pink bow in her hair.

"Thanks," said Hannah. "I designed it myself."

"I'll show you my dance," said Ruby.

She twirled around on her tiptoes, flapping her hands in the air.

"Stop showing off, Ruby," Chloe said, shooing her little sister away. "We need to plan what we're going to do for our science fair project." She sat down at the kitchen table, where she'd laid out notebooks, paper, sticky notes, marker pens, pencils and a stack of science books. "Right!" she said. "Let's get started."

Ellie wandered over to the window and peered out. "It's so sunny and warm. Let's work outside."

"Yes!" said Hannah. "That way the

dogs can play."

"Good thinking!" Peggy barked.

They gathered up all of Chloe's books and stationery and went outside.

"OK," Chloe began again, once everyone was sitting on the grass. "What topic should we pick—"

"It's too sunny," said Hannah, squinting. "Let's move to the shade."

They picked up their materials again and found a new spot, under a tree.

"Right," said Chloe. "Does anyone have an idea—"

BANG! BANG! BANG! The sound of hammering drowned out the rest of what she was saying.

"What's that noise?" asked Ellie.

"Finn's building a beehive in the garage," explained Chloe.

"Oooh!" said Ellie. "I want to see! I love building things too." She sprang up and ran into the garage. Hannah raced after her.

When they returned, Chloe tried one more time. "Let's make a list of things we can do for the science fair. Do you have any ideas, Hannah?"

Hannah shrugged. "Not really. I'm not very good at science." She began doodling on a piece of paper. Curious,

Peggy squeezed between the girls to see what she was drawing. It was a new outfit for Princess.

Ellie pulled Peggy on to her lap. "You're such a cutie," she cooed, tickling Peggy's tummy. "I wish I had a dog." Not wanting to miss out on the attention, Princess ran over and crowded on to Ellie's lap too. The two dogs wagged their tails, clamouring for more cuddles.

"Go and play," Chloe ordered Peggy and Princess. "We need to work."

Peggy reluctantly got up. She loved getting cuddles, but she could tell that

Chloe was starting to get annoyed.

"Race you to the vegetable patch!"
she barked, starting to run.

Princess bounded across the grass
after her. But when Princess got to
the vegetable patch she skidded to a

 stop, her fur
bristling.

Grrrrrrrrrr!
Princess
growled at
the scarecrow
robot.
The metal
contraption

moved its arms and Princess barked at it.

The girls ran over to see what was wrong.

"Don't be scared," soothed Hannah, stroking her dog. "It's just a scarecrow."

"That is so cool," said Ellie, going over to take a closer look at the robot.

"Finn built it for his science fair," said Chloe. "And speaking of that – we'd better get on with our project."

As the girls returned to their work, Princess and Peggy lay in the sunshine on the other side of the garden – keeping their distance from the scarecrow. Nearby, a bumblebee landed on a flower. Peggy watched it gathering nectar.

"Do you ever wish you were more important?" she asked her friend.

"What do you mean?" said Princess.

"Bees have an important job to do," said Peggy. "They make honey and pollinate plants. Dogs like us don't do anything important."

"Speak for yourself," said Princess. "I do something very important – I'm Hannah's muse."

"What does that mean?" asked Peggy.

"I give her inspiration," said Princess.

"Hannah wants to be a fashion designer when she grows up, and I give her ideas for what to make!" Princess stretched out on the grass and closed her eyes. "Now hush. A muse needs her beauty sleep."

Now Peggy felt even more worried. Even Princess had an important-sounding job! She watched the bumblebee flit from flower to flower. It didn't look too hard.

I could do that! thought Peggy, scrambling to her feet. *I can become a bumblebee!*

Peggy ran over to the flowerbeds and

dived into a big patch of geraniums.
Remembering what Chloe had said
about pollination, she rubbed her body
against the flowers, hoping that pollen
was sticking to her furry legs. Peggy
sniffed. Something was tickling her

nose. She moved

over to some

bright yellow

marigolds,

trampling

them with

her paws and

making clouds

of yellow pollen

float into the air. Now Peggy's nose tickled even more. Twitching her nose, Peggy went over to the pink peonies, and rubbed her whole body against the pretty flowers.

"Peggy!" called Chloe. "Get out of the flowerbed this instant!"

Peggy ran over to Chloe excitedly. She couldn't wait to show her friend all the pollen she'd collected. Just like a bumblebee.

"Look at me!" Peggy barked. "I'm a . . . a . . . a— *AAAAACHOOOO!*"

"Ew!" squealed the girls as Peggy sneezed all over them.

AAACHOOO!

AAACHOOOOO!

AAACHOOOOOOO!

Peggy's sneezes blew the sheets of paper the girls had been using into the air. Catching the breeze, they flew across the garden.

"Get them!" cried Chloe. She and her friends ran around the garden, grabbing paper from the flowerbeds and Dad's vegetable patch.

The commotion woke Princess up. "Ooh! This looks fun!" she barked. She pounced on a library book and bit it.

"Drop that, Princess," said Hannah, trying to pull the book out of her dog's mouth. But Princess wanted to have a tug of war.

"We'd better get back to work," said Chloe, when they'd finally gathered up their papers and wrestled the book away from Princess.

"Sorry," said Ellie, checking her watch. "I've got to get home for dinner."

"Me too," said Hannah.

"But what about our science fair

project?" said Chloe. "We haven't even agreed on a topic yet."

"Don't worry," said Hannah, clipping Princess's lead on to her collar. "We can get together next weekend."

"We still have loads of time," said Ellie.

But Chloe looked worried.

Peggy felt terrible. She knew how important this project was to Chloe. She'd messed things up yet again. Her plan to become a useful bumblebee hadn't worked – so she would just have to try harder!

Chapter Four

"When are the bees coming?" Chloe asked Dad, stirring a spoonful of honey into her porridge.

"Mr Apis said he'd drop them off mid-morning," said Dad.

Yay! thought Peggy, who was sitting by the table hoping that someone would drop some food on the floor. She couldn't wait to meet the bees. They might be able to give her some advice on how to become one of them.

"My friends are coming this afternoon to work on our science fair project again," said Chloe.

"They can stay for dinner if you like," said Mum, who was stirring something in a saucepan. "I'm making strawberry jelly for pudding."

"We still haven't picked a topic," said Chloe. "Do you have any ideas?"

"Sorry, sweetie," said Mum, shaking her head. "I'm a cook – not a scientist."

"Actually," said Dad, "cooking
is science. You're doing a science
experiment right now."

"What do you mean?" asked Mum.

"Well," explained Dad. "You're
making jelly with gelatin, which is
a protein. When you add it to warm

water, the bonds between the atoms weaken. But when it cools down, the protein chains become solid again."

"All I know is that it tastes good," said Mum, pouring the jelly into a mould shaped like a ring.

After breakfast, they went out to the garden. Finn came out of the garage carrying the beehive he'd made. "Where should we put it?" he asked.

"Not too close to Coco's hutch," said Chloe. "The buzzing might keep her awake."

"And not near the patio," said Mum, "because we eat out there sometimes."

"How about over here?" said Finn, setting the hive on the grass between the flowerbeds and the vegetable patch.

"Perfect," said Dad.

Peggy looked at the wooden box doubtfully. It didn't look very comfortable – or big enough for thousands of bees to share. Normally Peggy slept curled up next to Chloe on her warm, soft bed with its unicorn duvet. If she wanted to become a bee, she'd have to live in the hive. *I guess it might be fun having lots of roommates,* Peggy thought, though the hive didn't seem as nice as Chloe's cosy bedroom.

Not long afterwards, Mr Apis arrived in a van with the words Honey Valley Farm written on the side. He got out, wearing his white beekeeping suit, and opened the rear doors to remove a wooden box.

"Are the bees in there?" asked Ruby as Mr Apis carried the box around the side of the house and into the back garden.

"They sure are," said Mr Apis.

The farmer set the box down on the grass, near the hive Finn had built. Then he took out a metal contraption with a spout and handle. He placed the spout in the opening of the box and pumped the handle. A cloud of smoke puffed out. Peggy's nostrils twitched. She could smell fire!

"Get out!" barked Peggy, warning the bees. "Your house is on fire!"

Chloe looked concerned too, as smoke billowed around the hive. "Why are you doing that?" she asked Mr Apis.

"The smoke keeps the bees calm," explained the farmer. "When bees are scared, they release a scent that warns

all the other bees. But smoke interferes with their sense of smell, so they stay relaxed."

Peggy found the smell of smoke scary, but the bees didn't seem to mind it at all.

Mr Apis opened the lid of Finn's empty hive. Then he carefully opened his own hive and removed one of the wooden frames. It was covered in bees.

"Here's the queen bee," he said, holding up the frame to show the others. "There's only one per hive." Everyone crowded around to get a better look. The queen bee was hard to find, but eventually Peggy spotted a bee that was much larger than the others.

Ruby frowned. "Where's her crown?" she asked. "And her throne?"

"She doesn't have those things," said Mr Apis. "But make no mistake — she's still in charge of the hive. That's why I'm putting her in first. The other bees will follow the queen bee wherever she goes."

"Did she get picked to be the queen because she makes the most honey?" asked Chloe.

"She doesn't make honey," said Mr Apis. "Her job is to lay eggs like these."

He pointed to what looked like a white grain of rice embedded in the wax. "She can lay up to 1,500 eggs per day."

"So all the bees in this hive are her babies?" asked Chloe.

"That's right," confirmed Mr Apis.

Mum whistled softly. "That's a lot of kids to look after. I can barely keep up with my three."

"The queen has lots of help," said Mr Apis. "Most of the bees in the hive are worker bees. They work as a team. Everyone has a different job to do. Some go out and gather nectar, while others guard the hive. Some workers clean the hive, and others make royal jelly to feed the baby bees."

Ooh, thought Peggy. Royal jelly sounded fancy. And tasty!

Dad, who was wearing his new white beekeeper's suit, helped Mr Apis move the frames of bees into their new hive. Then they put the lid back on the hive.

Peggy wondered how the bees were feeling. When she had first come to live with Chloe's family, she had felt really nervous.

I'd better make them feel welcome, she thought.

"Hi, everyone," she barked, wagging her tail. "Welcome to your new home. You're going to love it here. Chloe and her family are really nice."

The bees flying in and out of the hive ignored her.

"What's your name?" she asked a bee that had landed on a daisy.

But the bee didn't reply.

"The vegetable patch is over there," Peggy barked, pointing with her paw. "And the flowerbeds are over there."

The bees didn't seem to need her help. They were already busy exploring the garden.

"Let me know if you want to play once you've got settled in," she barked.

Shortly after Mr Apis had left, Chloe's friends arrived to work on their science fair project. Peggy was disappointed that Hannah hadn't brought Princess this time. This time they didn't go outdoors. Once the girls were seated around the kitchen table, Chloe got straight down to business.

"I've been thinking – maybe we could do a project about flowers," said Chloe.

"I love flowers," said Hannah. "I'm sewing a dress with roses on it."

"Plants are boring," said Ellie. "I think we should build a robot, like the one

Finn made for his project."

"Oooh, that gives me an idea," said Hannah, sketching on her notepad. "I could make Princess a really cute robot outfit . . ."

"Try to focus, Hannah," Chloe said. "We really need to decide."

"OK," said Ellie. "Let's go for robots. Hannah thinks they're cool too."

"But she likes flowers too!" said Chloe, her hands on her hips. "And I don't want to copy my brother."

"Both ideas are fine with me," said Hannah, shrugging her shoulders.

"You're not helping," snapped Chloe.

"Well, you're being bossy," retorted Hannah.

Oh dear, thought Peggy, listening to Chloe and her friends squabble. They couldn't seem to agree on anything. Nobody was in charge. They needed someone to lead them.

Suddenly Peggy remembered what Mr Apis had said about the queen bee being in charge of the hive. If she became a queen bee, she could help organise Chloe and her friends. But how could she do that?

She looked around the kitchen, until her eyes landed on the jelly cooling in its mould on the counter.

Aha! Hadn't Mr Apis said something about royal jelly? Maybe if Peggy ate LOTS of jelly she would turn into a queen bee.

Chloe and her friends were too busy bickering to notice Peggy climb up on a chair. Placing her paws on the kitchen counter, she buried her face in

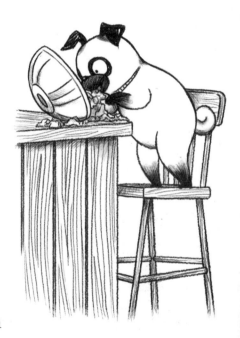

the wibbly-wobbly jelly and began to eat.

I wonder if royal jelly is strawberry flavoured too, she thought as she gobbled.

"Peggy!" exclaimed Chloe, staring at her in astonishment.

Have I turned into a bee already? Peggy wondered. She looked at her tummy. Her fur didn't have yellow and black stripes, but Chloe had shrieked so loudly that something must have worked.

"Listen up, girls," Peggy barked, hoping she sounded as regal as a queen bee. "You should do your science fair project on—"

"What have you done? That was supposed to be our pudding." Looking cross, Chloe picked Peggy up and set her down on the ground. "Naughty girl."

Peggy whimpered sadly. She hadn't meant to upset Chloe.

"We're getting nowhere," said Hannah, shutting her notepad. "I give up."

"I'm going home," said Ellie.

"Fine," said Chloe. Under her breath, she muttered, "I guess I'll just have to do it all by myself."

Oh dear, thought Peggy, licking jelly off her whiskers. She hadn't become a queen bee, or even a worker bee. And Chloe and her friends still hadn't agreed on a science project!

Chapter Five

"What are you doing?" Ruby asked Chloe, peering over her shoulder. Chloe was kneeling on the ground in the garden, planting sunflower seedlings in little pots.

"It's an experiment for the science fair," said Chloe. "I'm going to water these sunflowers with different liquids and see how that affects their growth."

"Isn't it supposed to be a group project?" asked Dad. He tossed some banana skins and eggshells on the compost heap, then turned it over with a garden fork.

"Yes," said Chloe. "But this is a great idea, so I decided to go ahead with it. I'm sure Ellie and Hannah will agree when I show them."

"I hope you're right . . ." said Dad, not sounding convinced.

Peggy pawed at Chloe and whined. It was the perfect day to play fetch or take a nice long walk.

"Sorry, Peggy," said Chloe. "I'm going inside to make a chart so I can track the sunflowers' growth."

Peggy looked around the garden. Ruby was twirling, skipping and leaping across the grass. It looked like a fun game, so Peggy ran over to join in.

"You're in the way, Peggy," complained Ruby. "I'm practising my dance routine for ballet class."

Peggy's ears pricked up as she heard Finn come out of the house, whistling. He headed towards the garage. Hoping he was getting his football out to go to the park, Peggy followed him into the garage.

But instead of picking up his football, Finn started pumping his bicycle tyres full of air.

"Sorry, Pegs," said Finn. "Me and my friends are going for a bike ride."

Leaving the garage, Peggy sighed. Mum was at the café, and everyone else was too busy to play with her. She glanced across the garden at the beehive. The bees had arrived two weeks ago, but she still hadn't managed to make friends with any of them, though she'd tried several times. They were always too busy working to talk to her.

Bored enough to play I Spy, Peggy wandered over to Coco's hutch, but the bunny was sleeping in her bed of wood shavings.

Peggy flopped down on the grass and buried her face in her paws.

"Come, come," said a little voice. "It can't be as bad as you think."

Peggy's head jerked up in surprise.

Who was talking to her?

"Over here!" called the voice. It was coming from a bee perched on a rosemary plant at the edge of the patio, where Mum grew herbs in pots.

"Oh, hello," said Peggy. "None of the other bees talk to me. They're all too busy making honey."

The bee laughed. "Well, I'm not a honeybee," she said. "I'm a bumblebee!"

"What's the difference?" asked Peggy.

"For starters," said the bee, "we're much friendlier! My name's Blossom, by the way."

"I'm Peggy," said Peggy. Now that

she thought about it, Blossom looked different from the bees who lived in the hive. She had the same yellow and black stripes as the honeybees, but her body was rounder and fluffier, like the pom-poms in Chloe's arts and crafts box.

"Honeybees aren't much fun," said Blossom. "It's all work and no play over in the hive. But we bumblebees are very social creatures."

"You don't live in the hive?" Peggy asked her new friend.

"Oh no," said Blossom. "I live somewhere much nicer – in a nest underneath the compost heap."

She pointed a wing over at the big pile
of rotting veg scraps and grass clippings
that Dad had made in one corner of the
garden.

"Oh . . ." said Peggy. Dad said

compost was good for the soil. But it was rather a stinky place to live!

"You know what they say," said Blossom cheerfully, beating her wings as she talked. "Location, location, location! It's a nice quiet neighbourhood, right next to the vegetable patch, and there are lots of wonderful places to eat nearby – have you tried the lavender?"

"Er, no," said Peggy.

Blossom gasped in shock. "No? It's gorgeous. You simply MUST try it!"

Peggy ran after Blossom as she buzzed across the garden. She was so happy to have finally made friends with a bee.

Hopefully Blossom could give her lots of advice on how to become a bumblebee!

Blossom landed on a stalk of lavender and buried her face in the purple flowers. "Delicious!"

Peggy sniffed the lavender doubtfully. The flowers didn't smell very tasty, but if that's what bees ate . . . Peggy nibbled on a stalk of purple flowers. *BLECH!* She spat it out on to the grass.

"Not keen?" said Blossom. "Oh well, all the more for us! Let me just tell the others!" Wings buzzing, she took off into the air.

Peggy followed Blossom over to the

compost heap, where several other bumblebees were buzzing around.

"Listen up, everyone," said Blossom. "This is Peggy. Peggy, meet everyone."

Then, as Peggy and the other bees watched, Blossom did something very strange. Waggling her bottom, she walked in a straight line, then circled around in a figure of eight, and did it again.

When Blossom had finished her strange routine, all the other bumblebees flew off in the same direction.

"Where are they going?" asked Peggy, feeling confused.

"To the lavender bush. My waggle dance is giving the others directions for where they can find some super-tasty nectar," explained Blossom. "That's how we bees communicate – by dancing."

Peggy suddenly had an amazing idea. "See you around, Blossom!" she barked. Then she bounded into the house through the patio doors. Chloe was working on her science project at the kitchen table.

"Look!" barked Peggy, waggling her bottom. "I'm a bumblebee!"

"What is it, Peggy?" asked Chloe. "Do you want to play?" She reached down and tossed a chew toy across the room.

Peggy ignored the toy and continued to waggle her bottom.

"Do you need a wee?" asked Chloe.

"No," barked Peggy. "I don't need a wee. I'm a BEE!" She waggled her bottom so hard she thought her tail might fall off!

Understanding dawned on Chloe's face. "Oh!" she said. "Now I get it!"

Finally! thought Peggy. *Chloe can tell that I've become a bumblebee!*

Standing up, Chloe went over to the door and fetched the lead hanging from the handle. "I've been so busy working on my project that I forgot to take you for a walk." She clipped the lead on to Peggy's collar. "Let's go to the park."

Peggy stopped waggling her bottom. Her bumblebee dance obviously needed some practice, but this wasn't a bad result. She was always happy to go for a walk with Chloe!

Chapter Six

Peggy and Chloe were in the garden.
Chloe had a ruler and was measuring
the height of her sunflowers, then
writing the numbers down on a chart.
It had been a week since she'd started
her experiment. Some of the sunflowers
looked strong and healthy, while others

looked rather droopy.

Peggy sniffed at one of the plants. Trying to act more like a bee, she cautiously nibbled one of the leaves. *YUCK!* Sunflowers tasted even worse than lavender!

"Hey! Stop eating my science project, Peggy," said Chloe. She stroked Peggy's head and gave her a kiss. "I don't want you to get a tummy ache."

Dad emerged from the house wearing his white beekeeping suit and holding the smoker. "How are your sunflowers coming along?" he asked Chloe.

Chloe checked her chart. "The ones

getting water are growing best," she
said. "And the ones getting coffee are
doing worst."

"Why aren't Ellie and Hannah
helping you?" asked Dad.

Chloe shrugged. "I haven't told them
yet," she said. "It's going to be a surprise.

They'll probably be glad I did all the work."

Dad went over to the hive and released a puff of smoke. He removed the hive's lid, then using a metal hook, he lifted out one of the frames.

"Is the honey ready to harvest?" Chloe asked.

Dad shook his head. "Not yet," he said. "They haven't made enough."

"I can't wait to taste it," said Chloe.

Peggy's mouth watered. *Me neither,* she thought.

"We need to be patient," said Dad, putting the frame back and replacing

the lid on the hive. Then he went over
to the vegetable patch to check on his
plants.

Maybe I can help, thought Peggy.
If she told the honeybees where they
could find some good nectar, they'd be
able to make more honey!

Moving her bottom, she practised the
dance she'd seen Blossom doing.

Waggle, waggle, waggle, then round in
a circle . . .

Waggle, waggle, waggle, then circle
the other way round.

She practised the dance until she was
sure she'd got it just right.

Peggy heard someone laughing. Looking up, she saw Tiger balancing on top of the fence. His green eyes sparkled with amusement as he watched her.

"Why are you shaking your body like that, Pig Tail?" Tiger asked. "Do you have fleas?"

"No, I do not!" she replied. Once a month, Chloe gave her medicine to prevent her from getting fleas and ticks. Peggy hated how the cold liquid felt on her fur but Chloe said it was to keep her healthy.

"So why are you acting like your tail is on fire?" said the cat.

"It's called a waggle dance," said Peggy. "It's how bees communicate with each other."

"I hate to break it to you, Pugly," said Tiger, "but you are not a bee."

Not yet, thought Peggy. *But I'm working on it.* "I'm going to tell the bees about the lavender bush. It has very good nectar." She started walking over to the beehive.

Tiger jumped down from the fence, blocking her way. "I wouldn't do that if I were you, Peggy," he said. "They don't need your help." For once he was using her real name, but Peggy didn't notice

Ugh! Tiger is so annoying! thought Peggy. She went around the cat. "It's OK," Peggy told him. "My friend Blossom showed me what to do."

Tiger shook his head. "Can't say I didn't warn you." Tensing his hind legs, he leapt back on top of the fence.

Peggy marched over to the beehive and began to do her dance. Concentrating hard, she moved forward, swinging her bottom from side to side. She ran around the beehive, and then repeated her dance – WAGGLE, WAGGLE, WAGGLE.

When she'd finished, she glanced around, disappointed not to see any bees flying over to the lavender bush she'd just told them about. But there were no bees in sight.

Of course, thought Peggy. They're all inside the hive!

She needed to get them to come out

so they could watch her dance. Peggy jumped up, resting her front paws against the hive. "Hello in there!" she called, sticking her snout into the entrance at the bottom. She could hear buzzing, so she knew the bees were at home. "Come out! There's something important I want to tell you—"

Something sharp jabbed her in the nose.

OUCH!

Then she felt it again – a sudden stab of pain, like she'd been poked in the face with a red-hot needle.

Peggy jerked her face away from the hive. A bee flew out.

"Help!" she yelped. "Something just—"

Before she could finish, the bee stung her on her paw.

"*OWWWWWWWWWW!*" Peggy howled in pain.

Suddenly, more bees flew out of the hive. Peggy ran away, but she was

outnumbered. Buzzing angrily, a swarm
of bees chased her around and around
the garden. Her face felt like it was on
fire!

"DAD!" shouted Chloe. "The bees are
attacking Peggy!"

Running over with his smoker, Dad
released puffs of smoke. Peggy coughed

as the bitter smell of smoke filled the air.
Finally, the buzzing stopped.

"Over here, Peggy!" called Chloe.

Peggy's eyes were streaming so badly
she couldn't see, but she followed the
sound of Chloe's voice.

"Oh, you poor, poor thing," said
Chloe, scooping Peggy up into her arms.

Painful red welts had sprung up all over Peggy's face. Her paw hurt too, where the bee had stung her.

As Peggy whimpered in Chloe's arms, she saw Tiger watching from the fence.

"I hate to say I told you so," he said, shaking his head. "But . . . I told you so."

Knowing that Tiger had been right was the most painful thing of all.

Chloe carried Peggy into the house. "Help!" she shouted. "Peggy's been stung by the bees."

"I'll call the vet," said Mum, getting out her phone.

Oh no! Not the vet, thought Peggy.

As Mum spoke to the vet, Chloe stroked Peggy. "It's going to be OK," she murmured.

Finn and Ruby crowded around to check on Peggy.

"Poor Peggy," said Finn. "Her face has swelled up like a balloon."

"I once got stung by a bee on my foot. It really hurt," said Ruby sympathetically.

Still on the phone, Mum came over and peered inside Peggy's mouth.

"What did the vet say?" asked Chloe after Mum had hung up.

"Peggy was lucky—" said Mum.

Lucky? thought Peggy. She didn't feel lucky at all!

"—the bees didn't sting her in her mouth, and she doesn't seem to have had an allergic reaction," continued Mum. "So we don't need to take her to the vet."

Phew! thought Peggy.

Dad hurried into the house, taking off his white hat. "What can we do to help?" he asked.

Like a queen bee telling the worker bees what to do, Mum took charge of the situation. "Chloe, keep Peggy still."

Chloe's arms tightened around Peggy.

Peggy instantly felt a bit better — she knew Chloe would look after her.

"Finn, please fetch me an ice pack," said Mum.

Finn hurried over to the freezer and took out an ice pack. He held it against Peggy's sore paw.

Ahhh, thought Peggy, closing her eyes. The cold felt nice and soothing.

"Ruby, darling, get me a jar of honey," said Mum.

Ruby quickly did what she was told. Mum dipped her finger in the honey and then dabbed it on the welts on Peggy's nose. "This should bring down

the swelling," she said.

A bit of honey slid down Peggy's nose.
Peggy licked it off. *SLURP!* The sweet

taste made her feel slightly better.

"The vet said we need to remove the stingers," said Mum.

As Chloe held out Peggy's paw, Dad used his fingernail to scrape out the stinger stuck in the pad.

OUCH! Peggy winced. But now the stinger was out, her paw smarted a bit less.

"Brave girl," crooned Chloe, stroking Peggy's back.

"Great work, team," said Mum.

Peggy snuggled into her friend's arms. She was starting to feel a bit better, but the bee stings had really hurt.

I don't want to be a bee any more, decided Peggy. Bees might be important, and their honey tasted sweet – but they weren't very nice at all!

Chapter Seven

Peggy trotted behind Chloe as she tended to her sunflowers. The sunflower that had been given water was taller than Peggy now. But the ones that had been getting watered with coffee and lemonade had only grown a few inches.

"I can't wait to show Ellie and

Hannah my sunflowers," said Chloe, noting down how much the plants had grown. "They are going to be so impressed."

A streak of orange fur leapt down from the fence and landed on the grass. Tiger strutted over to Peggy, the tip of his tail twitching.

Oh no, thought Peggy. He was going to tease her for being such an idiot.

Instead, Tiger said, "How are you feeling, Peggy?"

"Oh," said Peggy, surprised. She wasn't used to Tiger being nice to her. "I'm much better now. Thanks for trying to warn me. I wish I'd listened."

"That's OK," said Tiger. "When I was a kitten, I tried eating a bee. My whole tongue swelled up and I couldn't breathe. I nearly died."

"That sounds scary," said Peggy. She really had been lucky.

"Fortunately, cats have nine lives," said Tiger. He arched his back and winked. "Unlike stupid little dogs with curly-wurly tails."

Just like that, the old Tiger was back! He went over to a tree and started scratching the bark to sharpen his claws.

"Today's the day!" announced Dad,

coming outside in his beekeeping outfit, followed by Finn and Ruby.

"We're harvesting the honey!" said Finn.

"I'm helping!" said Ruby proudly.

"Ooh, that's exciting," said Chloe, setting down her watering can. "Can I help too?"

"Of course," said Dad.

Peggy gazed at the beehive warily. She'd been keeping her distance from the bees ever since she'd got stung. Her welts had faded and her nose was no longer swollen, but she could remember how much the stings had hurt.

"Hiya, Peggy," said a tiny voice. Blossom the bumblebee was sitting on one of Chloe's sunflowers.

Peggy cowered in fear. "Please don't hurt me!" she begged.

"Hurt you?" said Blossom. "Why would I do that?"

"I got stung by the bees from the hive," said Peggy. "And it REALLY hurt!"

"Ah," said Blossom. "Well, that's another big difference

between honeybees and bumblebees —
we bumblebees very rarely sting."

"But you DO sting sometimes," said
Peggy accusingly.

"Only when we're very frightened,"
said Blossom. "Did you do anything to
frighten the bees?"

Peggy thought about it. She had stuck
her nose in the beehive. She was just
being friendly, but she supposed it might
have looked a bit scary to the bees. After
all, she was a lot bigger than them.

"Maybe . . ." said Peggy. "But I didn't
mean to."

"Bees only sting when they're scared,"

explained Blossom. "It's our only way of defending ourselves." She flew over to the sweet peas, which grew on vines that twisted around bamboo canes arranged like a tepee. The bumblebee drank deeply from the flowers and gave a little burp. "Dee-licious! Want some? There's plenty to go round."

"Er, no thanks. I'm good," said Peggy. She'd had enough of trying to be a bumblebee. Or any sort of bee!

"Got to dash!" exclaimed Blossom. "I need to tell the others about these sweet peas." The bumblebee buzzed off towards the compost heap.

The smell of smoke wafted over from the other side of the garden. "Here we go," said Dad, setting the smoker down on the ground.

Peggy went over to join the others. She made sure not to get too close to the hive – she didn't want to scare the bees!

Dad took off the hive's lid and removed a frame. He brushed the bees off it, then carried the frame into the kitchen. Using a spoon, Dad scraped off a bit of the beeswax covering the frame. Golden honey oozed out from under the wax into a bowl.

"Look at that," Dad said approvingly. "Liquid gold."

Chloe stuck her finger in the honey and licked it off. "It tastes like flowers," she said.

Dad handed everyone a spoon. "Scrape the wax and honey into the bowl," he instructed them.

"Aren't the bees going to be upset that we're taking their honey?" asked Ruby.

"We'll leave plenty for them," said Dad, "so they can eat it in the winter, when there aren't many flowers around."

"That's ages away," said Chloe.

"Honey never goes off," said Dad. "Archaeologists once found honey in an ancient Egyptian tomb. It was over 3,000 years old, but amazingly you could still eat it."

"Eww," said Chloe. "I wouldn't eat that!"

"I'm surprised the mummies didn't eat it," joked Finn. "3,000 years is a long time to go without a snack."

Peggy's ears pricked up at the mention of snacks. She hadn't had a snack for ages either – at least three hours!

While the kids scraped honey and beeswax into the bowl, Dad went out to fetch more frames. After they'd finished scooping out all the wax and honey, Dad poured the runny golden mixture into a colander, placing a clean bowl underneath it. Honey oozed through the holes in the colander and dripped into the bowl. "This separates the wax from the honey," explained Dad.

"I can use the wax as wood polish," said Finn.

"I'm going to use some to make lip balms for my friends," said Chloe.

DRIP! DRIP! DRIP! The honey drained slowly into the bowl.

"There's a much quicker way to do this with a machine called a honey extractor," said Dad. "But those are expensive to buy."

"I bet I could make one," said Finn. "There's probably a video online showing how." He headed off to do some research on the computer.

Peggy's ears pricked up. Her hearing was much better than the humans', and she could hear footsteps outside. *WOOF! WOOF! WOOF!* she barked to alert the others.

A moment later – *DING DONG!* – the doorbell rang.

"See!" barked Peggy. "I told you someone was at the door."

"Shush, Peggy," said Chloe. "It's just Hannah and Ellie. I can't wait to show them my – I mean *OUR* – science experiment."

"We'll leave you in peace," said Dad. "Ruby and I are popping over to the café to see Mum."

Chloe came back into the kitchen with Hannah. But Ellie wasn't with her. Instead, she was with Princess, who was wearing a black and yellow striped jumper, and a headband with two black antennae with fluffy pom-poms on the ends of them.

Chloe clapped her hands in delight. "How adorable! Princess looks just like a bumblebee!"

Hannah pulled something stripy out of her bag. "I made one for Peggy too!"

As Chloe brought her sunflower plants in from the garden, Hannah dressed Peggy in her new outfit. Peggy tried to wriggle away, but Hannah wrestled her paws into the stripy jumper.

"Oh, Peggy, you look so cute!" said Chloe, setting her plants on the kitchen table.

Peggy didn't feel adorable. She felt silly. She didn't even want to be a bee any more!

The doorbell rang again. This time it

was Ellie, holding a big box.

"What's that?" asked Chloe.

"Ta da!" said Ellie, taking out a robot on wheels. "He's called Robbie. I built him from a kit and programmed him to be sound-activated." She set the robot down on the table.

Peggy climbed up on a chair and gave

the robot a suspicious sniff. Then Ellie
clapped her hands. The robot started
rolling forward. Ellie clapped her hands
again and Robbie stopped moving.

"Isn't he great?" said Ellie proudly.
"I'm sure we'll get an A for our science
project."

"Our project?" said Chloe. "That
isn't our project. THIS is our project!"
She gestured to the sunflowers and the
colourful charts which were spread
across the kitchen table. "I grew them
from seedlings and I've been feeding
them different liquids and measuring
their growth."

"That's boring!" said Ellie. "My robot is much better."

"This is a group project," said Chloe. "You weren't supposed to do the whole thing on your own."

"Isn't that exactly what you did?" demanded Ellie.

Chloe turned to Hannah. "You need to decide which project we use," she said.

"Um . . . they're both really good . . ." said Hannah. "I don't want to pick one."

"Typical!" said Ellie. "You haven't done anything on this project!"

"I was busy making the bumblebee

outfits," Hannah protested.

"This is a disaster," Princess said to Peggy.

Peggy shook her head in dismay. Chloe and her friends hadn't listened to each other. They had each done their own thing, without thinking of the group. And now the girls were arguing again! Peggy wished she could do something to get the girls' friendship – and their science project – back on track.

They need to be more like bees, she suddenly realised. Bees worked together as a team. Peggy had failed at becoming a queen bee once before — but SOMEONE had to sort out the girls. She looked the part now, so she would have to try becoming a bee again.

"Stop fighting!" barked Peggy.

But the girls carried on bickering.

"This is all your fault!" said Chloe.

"No!" said Ellie. "It's your fault!"

"STOP!" barked Peggy, as loud as she could.

WHIRRRRR! Peggy's bark made Robbie start moving. The robot marched along the kitchen table and crashed into the bowl of honey, knocking it over. Sticky golden honey spilled all over Chloe's beautiful charts.

"Noooo!" howled Chloe. She picked up her honey-covered charts and tried to wipe the honey off but it was no use. They were ruined.

The robot carried on trundling through the puddle of honey. Ellie dived to rescue her robot, but she accidentally knocked it off the table.

CRASH! Robbie fell on the floor in a jumble of cogs and gears.

"Robbie's broken!" wailed Ellie. She gathered up the bits that had fallen off her robot and reattached them. Setting

Robbie on the floor, she clapped her hands. The robot took a few steps. There was a spluttering noise, then Robbie came to a juddering halt.

"Maybe Finn can help you fix it?" said Chloe.

Ellie picked the robot up and shook her head. "The honey damaged the motor."

"What are we going to do?" asked Hannah. "The science fair is tomorrow."

"We'll need to start again," said Ellie.

"But we don't have an idea," said Chloe.

Luckily, Peggy did have an idea.

A very good idea. She knew exactly what the girls should do their science project on. But could she get them to understand?

Chapter Eight

"Follow me," Peggy told Princess. "And do what I do." She ran outside and started waggling her bottom, barking to attract attention. Princess copied her. The two dogs in bumblebee outfits ran in a figure of eight around the beehive, barking and waggling their tails.

The girls came outside to see what was going on.

Please let Chloe understand what I'm trying to tell her, thought Peggy.

There was a long pause as the girls stared at the dancing dogs in confusion, and then—

"BEES!" shouted Chloe. "We can do our science fair project on bees!"

Yes! thought Peggy. The waggle dance had worked!

"That's a great idea," said Ellie. "I can't believe we didn't think of that before."

"I love bees," said Hannah. "They're really cute."

"Finally," said Chloe. "Something we can agree on!"

The girls went inside and cleaned

the sticky honey off the table. Chloe threw her ruined charts in the bin and took her plants back outside. Peggy and Princess helped by lapping up honey from the floor.

"Shame Robbie is broken," joked Ellie. "He could have helped us clean up."

"Robbie was a really clever invention," said Chloe. "I'm sorry I was being so stubborn."

Ellie shook her head. "I'm sorry too. I didn't listen."

"And I'm sorry I didn't help out enough," said Hannah.

The friends hugged.

"Aww," said Princess. "Humans are so cute."

Peggy wagged her curly tail in agreement. She was happy to see Chloe and her friends getting along again.

"We can still do an awesome science fair project," said Ellie.

"But this time we need to work as a team," said Chloe. She checked her watch. "We don't have a lot of time, but if we each have a job, we should be able to get everything done."

"I can make a model of a bee," said Ellie.

"That sounds great," said Chloe. "I've

been reading lots of books about bees, so I can write a presentation."

"I can design a poster," said Hannah. Taking out her marker pens, she started drawing a picture of a beehive.

The girls got down to work, each concentrating on their own job. For hours, the only sounds were the rustle of turning pages and the squeaking of marker pens against card.

"I see there's been a change of plans," said Dad, when he and Ruby returned home from the café.

When the girls explained what had happened, Dad offered to help. He picked samples of bee-friendly plants from the garden, so that Hannah could draw them on her poster. Finn helped, too. He looked up bee facts on the internet for Chloe's presentation. Ruby helped Hannah glue black and yellow pompoms on to the bee model. Then they used pipe cleaners to make legs and antennae.

"Want to see my dance now?" Ruby asked when they'd finished.

"Don't bother the girls," said Dad. "They still have a lot of work to do."

But Chloe was staring at her little sister. "Ruby, you're a genius!" she said.

"I am?" said Ruby.

"Yes!" said Chloe. "I've just been reading about how bees communicate with each other by doing a special dance."

I could have told you that, thought Peggy.

"We could do a dance as part of our presentation," said Chloe. "To show how bees tell each other where to find pollen."

Hannah's eyes lit up. "I love that idea."

"Me too!" said Ellie enthusiastically.

They went outside and Chloe demonstrated the bee waggle dance.

"Walk in a line and wiggle your bum," she said. "Then go around in a figure of eight."

Giggling, the girls all shook their bottoms as they danced around the garden.

"Science is actually pretty fun," said Hannah, laughing.

"Do you think we'll get a good grade?" asked Chloe.

"I'm not sure," said Ellie. "Maybe we still need something else . . ."

"I've got it!" said Hannah. "Princess and Peggy should be part of our presentation. They can wear their bee outfits."

"What do you say, Peggy?" asked Chloe. "Do you want to be part of our team?"

"Yes!" Peggy woofed, wagging her tail. Nothing would make her happier!

The science fair was held in the school
hall the following evening. Chloe and
Hannah had got special permission
from Miss Jenkins, their teacher, to bring
their dogs along. Peggy went with her
family, wearing her bee outfit.

"Hi, Princess," she greeted her friend.

"Honestly," Princess said. "What
would these people do without our
help?"

Tables were set up around the hall to
display the children's science projects.
Parents, siblings and teachers went from

table to table, listening to the children's presentations, asking questions and admiring the experiments.

Peggy watched a boy pour vinegar into the top of a volcano made of papier-mâché. Froth fizzed out of the top, running down the side of the volcano like lava.

"Wow!" said Ruby.

"Someone in my year did that exact same experiment," said Finn, unimpressed.

One group had grown sparkling crystals. Another group demonstrated a battery made from a lemon. Then they

came to a group who had studied the
life cycle of a frog. Their poster showed
how eggs grew into tadpoles, and then
became frogs.

"My neighbours gave us some
frogspawn from their pond," explained
a girl with glasses. "And we watched
them grow into these adult frogs." She
reached into a tank and took out a frog.

The frog wriggled out of her hands
and hopped across the hall. "Freedom!"
it cried, as people squealed and jumped
out of the way. Peggy was too excited
about the presentation to bother
chasing after it.

"There they are!" said Ruby, pointing to the very last station.

Hannah's poster looked beautiful, Ellie's bee model was very realistic and Chloe's presentation was full of interesting facts and information. Peggy was so proud of the girls – not just because their science project looked so impressive, but because they had finally figured out how to work as a team.

The girls stepped out from behind their table.

"We're now going to show you how bees communicate with each other," said Chloe. "With a little help from our

dogs, Peggy and Princess."

Mum unclipped Peggy's lead, and Peggy took her place next to Chloe and her friends.

The girls and dogs did their waggle dance.

"The distance the bee dances tells the others how far away the flowers are," said Ellie.

"And the longer the dance goes on for, the better the flower patch they've found," added Hannah.

Everyone clapped when they finished their presentation.

"I'm giving you all an A plus," said

Miss Jenkins, when they'd finished. She crouched down to pet the dogs. "Peggy and Princess get top marks as well."

"Yay!" cried the girls.

"Go us!" said Chloe, giving her friends high fives.

When the science fair was over, Chloe walked home with her family.

"Congratulations," said Mum. "You girls did a great job."

"And wasn't it better doing it as a team?" asked Dad.

Chloe nodded. "Thanks for your help,

everyone," she said. Crouching down, Chloe picked up Peggy. "Especially you."

That's OK, thought Peggy, licking Chloe's cheek. *We're a team.* She would do anything for her best friend.

"You're the best, my little bumblebee," said Chloe, grinning.

Within her stripy jumper, Peggy's heart swelled with pride. She might not be able to make honey like a real bee, but she could make Chloe smile – and that was the sweetest thing in the whole world!

The End

Coming soon!

A bewitching new story starring Peggy the pug!

A mischievous kitten has moved in next door and is causing mayhem . . . Can Peggy become a witch and magic her pesky new neighbour away?

The Pug who wanted to be a Witch

Have you read all of
Peggy the pug's adventures?

The Pug *who wanted to be a* Unicorn

Bella Swift

The Pug *who wanted to be a* Reindeer

Bella Swift

The Pug *who wanted to be a* Bunny

Bella Swift

The Pug *who wanted to be a* Pumpkin

Bella Swift

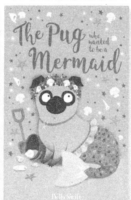

The Pug *who wanted to be a* Mermaid

Bella Swift

The Pug *who wanted to be a* Star

Bella Swift

The Pug *who wanted to be a* Fairy

Bella Swift

The Pug *who wanted to be an* Elf

Bella Swift